ROWAN TREE STABLES

Ride to the Rescue

ROWAN TREE STABLES

Ride to
the Rescue

Nina Carberry

WITH JULIE SYKES

ILLUSTRATED BY
NUNO ALEXANDRE VIEIRA

GILL BOOKS

Gill Books
Hume Avenue
Park West
Dublin 12
www.gillbooks.ie

Gill Books is an imprint of M.H. Gill and Co.

Text © Nina Carberry 2023
Illustrations © Nuno Alexandre Vieira 2023

9780717198719

Designed by Bartek Janczak
Print origination by Sarah McCoy
Printed and bound in Great Britain
by CPI Group (UK) Ltd, Croydon, CRO 4YY
This book is typeset in Georgia.

*The paper used in this book comes from the wood
pulp of sustainably managed forests.*

A CIP catalogue record for this book is available
from the British Library.

5 4 3 2 1

For Ted , Rosie and Hollie

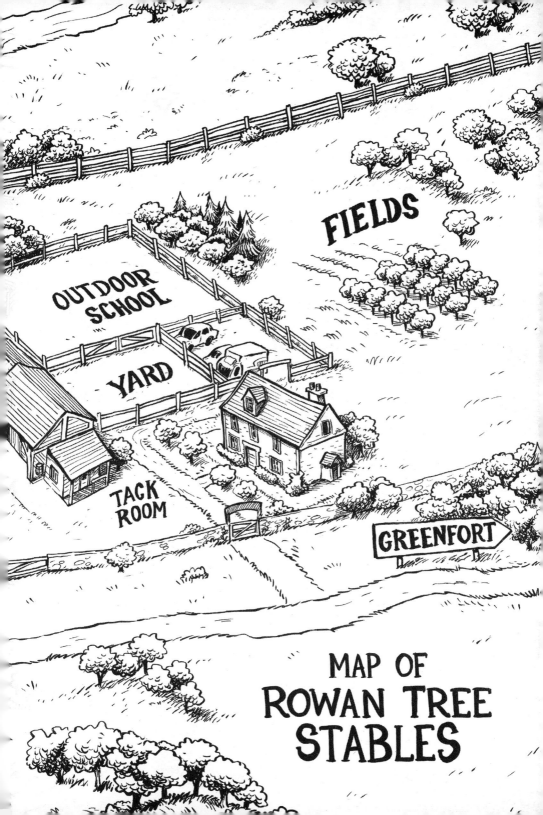

Chapter 1

'Here comes Daisy Dynamite! She's coming up fast and she's overtaking Noble Nipper ...'

Grace pretended she was galloping a racehorse as she cycled through the gates into Rowan Tree Stables. Pedalling furiously, she came up alongside her best friend, Aaron, as they passed Rowan House, home to her grandparents, Denis and Una O'Brien. They owned

1

the stables and were the reason Grace loved riding so much. Denis had lived in Rowan House his whole life. He had sat Grace on a pony before she could even walk, and when she'd turned six he'd taught her to ride. She'd ridden at Rowan Tree Stables ever since.

'Noble Nipper makes a comeback, it's Noble Nipper and Daisy Dynamite, neck and neck!' screamed Aaron, imitating his favourite racing commentator.

They hurtled into the yard on their bikes, Aaron's jacket flapping, Grace's long brown plait flying out behind her.

'It's a dead heat. Daisy Dynamite and Noble Nipper win the Irish Grand National!' Grace yelled, punching the air as Aaron cheered wildly.

They were still laughing as they parked up behind the tack room, hanging their cycle helmets off their handlebars.

'Saturday, my favourite day of the week!' said Grace as they walked over to the pony barn.

'Mine too,' said Aaron, pushing his blond fringe out of his eyes. 'No school for two whole days!'

Ten-year-olds Grace Ryan and Aaron Collins went to different schools but had become friends through the local triathlon club. They liked to challenge each other – whether running or riding, they were equally competitive!

As they stepped inside the barn, Grace inhaled deeply, filling her lungs with the sweet smell of horse and straw.

The pony barn had twenty stables, ten on either side, with a wide walkway down the middle.

Grace hurried along the left-hand side to a stable where Daisy, a pretty, grey Connemara pony with a proud, white face, was looking out. Daisy stamped a hoof and whickered as Grace approached. Grace's heart flipped with happiness. Granny and Grandad had bought Daisy for her not long after she'd learnt to ride. Although Daisy had to earn her keep at the riding school by taking part in lessons, and Grace was expected to help out too, Daisy was Grace's very own pony, and their relationship was special. Grace sometimes got a little anxious and jealous when other children rode Daisy. But Grandad only put experienced riders on her, and none of them shared the same special bond that Grace and Daisy had.

Aaron loved horses too, but his family didn't have any spare money for riding lessons, let alone to buy him a horse. So when Grace had suggested he help out at Rowan Tree Stables in return for rides, he'd jumped at the chance. Now, when they weren't at triathlon club, Grace and Aaron spent all their free time at the stables.

Daisy whinnied impatiently. Grace slipped inside the stable, wrapping her arms around the pony's soft neck and hugging her. Daisy rubbed her head against Grace's arm before pulling away and nuzzling her with velvety lips.

'Looking for a treat, are you?' Grace giggled as Daisy became more insistent, shoving her nose against the pocket of Grace's jodhpurs, trying to get at the mints she knew Grace always carried.

Grace gave her a mint and Daisy hoovered it up. In the stable opposite, Aaron was offering his favourite pony, Nipper, some nuts. At 13.2 hands, Nipper was the same height as Daisy. The resemblance ended there. Daisy, who loved her food, was a round-bellied pony with a wavy, light-grey mane and tail and two white socks. Skewbald Nipper was leaner and more athletic-looking. His brown mane turned blond towards his withers, and he had a long, brown tail.

Nipper was a fussy eater, and he eyed Aaron's pony nuts suspiciously, his lips twitching. Daisy had no such concerns and gobbled up all the mints.

'All gone.' Even when Grace showed Daisy her empty hands, the pony nudged at her pocket for more. 'I've got an apple I'll share with you later. I've work to do now.' Grace smoothed down Daisy's mane, patting her on the neck before reluctantly letting herself out of the stable. She'd just bolted the door behind her when Gabriela, a student instructor from Spain, arrived.

'*Hola!* Did you two even go home last night? You are always first here and last to leave!' Gabriela's brown eyes crinkled with amusement as she approached. 'Grace, your grandad wants to see you both. He's in the tack room.'

Grace was intrigued. This sounded important. If Grandad had something to say, he usually came and found them himself.

Aaron frowned. 'Are we in trouble?' he asked.

Gabriela raised an eyebrow. 'Do you *think* you're in trouble?'

Grace ran through the jobs they'd been given yesterday after school. Refilling the water buckets. Tick. Cleaning the tack. Tick. Sweeping up the hay from the split bale. Tick. *And* they'd remembered to put the broom back. She was pretty sure they weren't in trouble. Unless ... in a rush she remembered the water fight she'd started with Aaron when they'd been filling buckets. It had been lashing rain, they were already very wet and there were no clients in the yard at the time. Surely they weren't in trouble for that?

'I don't think so ...' she ventured.

From the look on Aaron's face, he had remembered the water fight too. 'Denis isn't going to stop me from helping out, is he?' he stuttered.

'No! It's nothing like that,' said Gabriela. 'You two are our best helpers! You and Grace turn up every day, no matter the weather.

I was just teasing you. Stop imagining the worst and go and see him.'

Grace rubbed her hands down her jodhpurs and rearranged her plait, pushing it back over her shoulder. Aaron ran his hands through his hair too, but only managed to make his blond mop look even messier. *Not that Grandad would notice*, Grace thought, shooting Aaron a reassuring smile. The only thing Grandad insisted on was the right clothes for the job – that and making sure his horses were properly turned out and looked after. Watch out if you took an ungroomed pony out for a lesson or ride!

'What do you reckon this is about?' said Grace curiously as they hurried next door to the tack room.

Aaron shrugged his shoulders.

As they went inside, Grace almost fell over Rocky, who had snuck up from behind, rushing between her legs to drop a ball at her feet. The Jack Russell terrier crouched in front of her, his tail wagging so fast his whole body shook.

Grandad looked up from sorting through some headcollars and growled, 'Rocky, stop that, you scamp, lie down.'

Not a chance! Grace thought, bending to pat the little dog. Rocky licked her hand, then jumped at her legs before running over to say hello to Aaron. Rolling onto his back, the terrier waved his paws in the air, inviting Aaron to rub his belly.

Grace straightened up. 'Hiya, Grandad, you wanted to see us?'

'I did indeed,' Grandad replied. Then, turning to Aaron and grinning kindly, he said, 'Don't look so worried, boy. You aren't in trouble, unless there's something you're not telling me?'

Grace felt a rush of affection. Grandad was the kindest person ever and brilliant at putting people and animals at ease.

'Granny and I were talking last night. You've been riding out together for a while now. You handle your ponies well, you've both got good heads on you, and there've been no disasters. Gabriela tells me you've worked hard at jumping. You're confident and, more importantly, you respect the ponies. I know you both love going to the Furzebush Field to jump, so Granny and I have decided that from now on you can go up there together, without an adult.'

'No way!' Grace squealed, and then did a little jig before throwing herself at Grandad and hugging him tightly. 'Grandad, that's class!'

'Yesss!' said Aaron, his eyes sparkling. 'Thanks a million, Denis.'

'No need to thank me,' Grandad said, untangling himself from Grace. 'You've both earned the privilege. One rule applies, though. No riding alone. Not for any reason. You go together or not at all.'

'Always,' said Grace. 'Daisy and Nipper both have lessons this morning. We'll be riding them after lunch. Can we go to the Furzebush Field then?'

'You can,' said Grandad. 'Now, off with the pair of you. There's lots of work to get through first!'

'We're on it!' Grace couldn't stop grinning as she and Aaron left the tack room.

Chapter 2

Grace hated waiting for things but luckily, even though she had thought the morning would drag, the time flew by. Saturday was the riding stables' busiest day. While Gabriela fed the ponies, Grace and Aaron set to work refilling water buckets. By then the kids who helped on Saturdays had arrived and pitched in with the mucking out and grooming.

The ponies needed for the first lesson were being tacked up when a stream of cars came along the drive.

'Rocky, come back!' Grace grabbed the little dog to stop him from dashing across the yard to chase the arriving vehicles as they swung into the car park.

Saturday morning lessons were mostly for younger children, and they gathered outside the pony barn now, chattering excitedly. Grace and Aaron helped them to mount, tightening girths and adjusting stirrup lengths, and then led them up to the outdoor sand school. Then they brought Storm, a bay gelding, and Merlin, a dun, in from the field for Grandad and a friend to ride out. They washed mud from the horses' legs, and then Grace tacked up Storm, Grandad's horse, while Aaron saw to Merlin.

At lunchtime, Grace and Aaron sank gratefully down on a straw bale in the large open space between the tack room and the hay barn to eat their sandwiches. Rocky joined them, fixing them with an intense stare as he sat at their feet, hoping for a share of their food.

'Gently,' said Aaron, feeding Rocky cheese from his sandwich.

'Paws off my apple, I'm sharing it with Daisy.' Grace shoved it back in her lunchbox as Rocky wolfed down the cheese and then jumped into her lap to see what else she had.

With their food eaten, they set to work getting the ponies ready for Gabriela's afternoon lesson. Grace and Aaron could hardly contain their excitement as they led the ponies into the yard.

They loved all of them, they were each such characters. Grace took Bear, a hairy, piebald Irish Cob who was every bit as soft and cuddly as his name and a big favourite at the stables.

'Is Primrose being a diva?' she asked, chuckling as the light-gold palomino mare forced Aaron to take a detour around a puddle.

'Total diva,' said Aaron. 'She doesn't want to get her hooves wet!'

'Steady, Bonnie,' Gabriela spoke gently to the strawberry roan she was leading. Bonnie, a mistress of escape, was shaking her head as she tried to rid herself of the bridle. Headcollar, bridle or even her stable, Bonnie saw each of them as personal challenges to free herself from!

When Gabriela finally led the mounted riders away to the outdoor sand school, Grace and Aaron high-fived. They raced to the tack room, where they swapped wellies for riding boots and put on helmets and back protectors. They couldn't wait to

go jumping in the Furzebush Field. It was the best spot for practising cross-country riding, with fallen tree trunks and big furze bushes. In record time, Daisy and Nipper were tacked up and ready to go. Using the mounting block, Aaron lightly swung himself into Nipper's saddle. He then moved away to adjust his stirrups, making space for Daisy and Grace. 'How do you want to get there?' he asked. 'Shall we take the greenway?'

Once a working railway line that connected the nearby town of Greenfort to Dublin, the greenway ran alongside the boundary of Rowan Tree Stables. The riding school used the greenway a lot as a safe and traffic-free route to get to the woods and gallops beyond.

'Let's ride across the fields. It's quicker, and there'll be more time for jumping,' replied Grace.

'Grand,' said Aaron, picking up his reins and asking Nipper to walk on.

They rode over to the fields, chatting happily as they went. Grace pushed Daisy into a trot and then a canter.

'Come on, girl,' Grace called, urging her pony on with her legs. Suddenly a bird flew up from a bush, startling Nipper, who swerved into Daisy.

'Whoa! Steady there!' Taken by surprise, Grace lost both stirrups and tipped forward onto Daisy's neck.

'Sorry!' Aaron sat deep in the saddle, talking to Nipper in a soothing voice as the pony shied again.

Grace clung on to Daisy's mane as her pony jumped out of Nipper's way. She wriggled back into the saddle, her feet searching for the stirrups.

Nipper's ears flickered. He threw his head up and pranced backwards. Calmly, Aaron nudged him forwards, but still Nipper edged back.

Grace called out, 'I'll ride on ahead. He might settle if he's following Daisy.'

Daisy's ears went back. She wasn't so keen on taking the lead, and Grace was surprised at how firmly she had to push her pony on. 'I guess Nipper's spooked her,' she said. 'They're not used to us riding out alone.'

'I thought you were coming off. You were like a bushbaby clinging on to Daisy's neck!' Aaron couldn't help grinning

Grace chuckled. 'It wasn't my best riding. Good thing Grandad's not here to see! Let's just take it easy for a bit.'

The ponies settled at last, and soon they were cantering across the fields happily. The ponies waited patiently at each of the gates while Grace and Aaron opened and closed them. Grace's heart leapt as she caught sight of the Furzebush Field, its prickly bushes with bright yellow flowers resembling bursts of sunshine ahead of her. Now Nipper fought for his head, seeing the jumping field and wanting to gallop to it. From the smile on his face, Grace knew that Aaron was loving the challenge of riding the flighty pony.

'Want to let them go?' she called.

'Sure,' said Aaron.

The horses surged forward, snorting as they galloped. Their manes caught the wind and flowed behind them as their riders urged them on. Finally, breathless and laughing, Grace and Aaron pulled their ponies up.

'That was deadly!' said Grace, patting Daisy as she rode through the gap in the stone wall surrounding the Furzebush Field. 'And this is my all-time favourite place.'

'Mine too. Did I tell you I saw an otter in the river over there last week? Dad and I were cycling on the greenway.'

Grace rolled her eyes. 'Only about a thousand times.'

Aaron grinned back, too good natured to take her seriously. 'It was eating a fish. It was holding it in its paws—'

'It ate the whole thing, even the tail, and afterwards it groomed its face to clean its fur. Yep, you said that too!' Grace feigned a yawn. 'Same course as usual, or shall we make up a different one?'

'Let's stick with what we know, since this is our first time jumping without grown-ups,' said Aaron.

'OK.' Aaron was an excellent rider, but he was a little more cautious than Grace. 'Will I go first?' she said.

Aaron nodded, and Grace walked Daisy over to their imaginary start line by the wall. Grace's eyes narrowed as she scanned the course. Daisy tossed her head, impatient to get going. Grace turned the pony away from the start before trotting back over it and pushing Daisy on down the side of the field until they were almost at the greenway and the woods and river beyond it.

Swinging Daisy round to the right, Grace glanced over at the first jump, a small gorse bush, compact and bursting with flowers. 'Ready, girl?'

Giving Daisy her head, Grace set off at a canter, rising forward into jumping position as they approached the bush. Daisy jumped high, clearing it with ease.

'Well done!' Grace patted her pony's neck and then swung right to canter diagonally back up the field. Halfway up they met the second furze, this one larger than the first. A soft breeze brushed Grace's cheeks, and her tummy swooped as Daisy soared upwards, clearing the bush with room to spare. The pony landed neatly, clods of grass flying from her hooves, before she galloped on. Grace checked her, holding her back to make one last turn, then giving Daisy her head as they galloped towards the fallen tree trunks in the middle of the field.

Aaron whooped as Daisy and Grace cleared them all, sailing over the final bush and galloping a short way before slowing. 'Clear round! Next stop, the RDS!'

'I didn't get my toes prickled once,' shouted Grace, patting Daisy's neck.

'My turn!' Aaron barely waited for Grace to pull Daisy to a halt before he was off, riding a prancing Nipper over to the start of the course.

Grace kept Daisy on a short rein as she watched them jump, willing Nipper on, hoping the pony wouldn't refuse at the final bush as he had last time they'd jumped here with Gabriela. But Nipper was on fire, and Grace could see the concentration on Aaron's face as he steered the pony over each jump at a fast canter.

'Yaaaay!' she cheered as Nipper cleared the last bush without hesitation and galloped back up the home straight.

'That was awesome!' Aaron glowed with happiness as he brought Nipper alongside her. 'Jumping on our own, no adults watching and telling us what to do, is my new favourite thing.'

'Mine too,' Grace agreed.

They rode round the field more slowly, jumping bushes here and there until Daisy began to sweat and

Grace pulled up. 'Shall we let them cool off by the river?'

'Good plan. Let's go to the shallow bit where they can get a drink.' Aaron led the way out of the field, across the greenway and through the trees until they reached the water.

They dismounted, ran up their stirrups and loosened the ponies' girths. Then, looping the reins over their ponies' heads, they led them down to the water, where both animals had a drink.

'Looks like no otters today,' said Grace as they hung around on the bank, letting the ponies cool down. Daisy immediately began snacking on the grass, but Nipper took longer to settle, his ears twitching suspiciously at the gurgling river and every rustle or snap that came from the bushes and trees.

Grace checked her watch. 'We don't have to be back for a while. Will we ride along the greenway through the woods?'

Aaron agreed, his eyes on the river, no doubt still watching for his otter.

Grace went over and tightened Daisy's girth and lengthened her stirrups again. She gathered the reins and was about to mount when Aaron came alongside her and whispered urgently in her ear.

'Grace, look over there, quick!'

Chapter 3

Grace swung round. 'What's up?'

'It's the otter,' whispered Aaron. 'See the bush nearest the river, it's underneath it.'

At first glance, Grace didn't see anything, but when she looked more carefully she could just make out an animal with a small head, rounded ears and bright, inquisitive eyes crouching under the bush. The otter's nose twitched, then suddenly it broke cover. It was larger and much cuter than Grace had expected, with thick, grey-brown fur, a broad snout and a black button nose with long whiskers. Its feet were webbed, and it had a long tail. It scampered towards the riverbank, stopping halfway. Grace and Aaron stayed very still. The otter stared around, its whiskers twitching as it sniffed the air. Finally, it let out a sharp squeak.

'Look!' Grace gasped as three otter pups slithered from under the bush and scampered after their mam.

The first two pups were much bigger than the last one. They ran past their mother, squeaking excitedly as they slid into the river. The smallest pup stopped on the bank and peered uncertainly at the water. The pup was looking as if it was going to return to the bush when its mam came up behind and nudged it impatiently. The pup squeaked and, planting its paws in the ground, refused to budge. The otter shoved it again, knocking the pup over.

'Go on!' said Grace, willing the pup to try the water, but it scrambled up and ran away.

The big otter gave chase and, catching the pup up, she clamped her mouth on the back of its neck. Unceremoniously, she dragged it back to the river and, using her nose, pushed it into the water.

The pup disappeared in a ring of bubbling ripples. Now Grace could hardly bear to watch, certain that the pup would drown but knowing there was nothing she could do about it. Grandad, who loved nature and managed his fields so they were wildlife-friendly, had taught her that in most cases it's better to leave wild animals alone and only try to help them if they're badly injured.

The water bubbled, and a grey-brown head broke through the surface. The otter pup stared around. Then, spotting its siblings, it paddled frantically in their direction.

'Would you look at that!' whispered Aaron.

Grace couldn't stop smiling. She tried to imagine her dad throwing her in the water when she was learning to swim. He hadn't, of course, but she wouldn't have put it past Finn, her annoying big brother, to try it!

Watching the pups playing happily, paddling about and chasing each other in wide circles, Grace finally understood why Aaron hadn't stopped talking about the otters. They were magical creatures, and the pups were so cute, splashing around in the river together.

Daisy was growing restless. Glancing around, she spied a lush clump of grass near the water's edge. Shaking her head, she stepped towards it. The jingle

of her bridle broke the silence. The mother otter's
head whipped round to Grace, Aaron and the ponies.
Quickly, she rounded her pups up and shooed them
over to the riverbank. The littlest
pup needed no encouragement this
time. Sensing danger, it slithered
out of the water and chased its family back to the
safety of the bush.

'Steady, girl,' Grace said, checking Daisy and
stopping her from wandering over to the grass.

'Daisy, you bold pony!' Aaron was disappointed.

'Sorry!' Grace apologised.

'There must be an otter holt under that bush. An
otter digs an underground burrow to have her pups in.
I'm going to come back with Dad. He'd love to see them.'

'Grandad would too,' said Grace. 'Shall we ride
on for a bit? We've enough time.'

'Sure.' With a final glance at the bush, Aaron
looped Nipper's reins back over the pony's head and
looked about for somewhere to mount.

There was a handy boulder at the edge of the greenway, and they used that before joining the trail. They rode on through the woods, occasionally catching glimpses of the river through the trees. Grace felt so happy she thought she might burst. Today had been the best day ever. Jumping Daisy, her favourite pony in the whole wide world, in the Furzebush Field with her closest friend. Life didn't get much better!

Grace and Aaron rode on in a companionable silence until Aaron suddenly said, 'Will you look at that!'

'What?' Grace stared around her.

'There, through the trees.'

Grace let out a gasp as she saw what Aaron was pointing at. 'Oh no! What's happened?'

At first glance, it looked like some kind of tornado had ripped through the wood, creating a clearing where tree after tree had toppled from their roots. On closer inspection, Grace could see that the trees had not fallen accidentally but had been deliberately felled.

Tree trunks were stacked one on top of the other beside an enormous pile of branches and leaves. Bushes had been ripped up and left in another heap, with their roots reaching out like grasping fingers. Further along was a second pile of trunks, which towered over Grace and Daisy. Everywhere they looked the muddy earth was covered with sawdust, creating a landscape that reminded Grace of pictures she'd seen of the moon's surface. The tree felling covered the square patch of land that bordered the river.

'Who did this?' Grace said, pulling Daisy up and staring around in disbelief. 'Why have they hacked everything down? That's terrible!'

'Not necessarily,' said Aaron. 'Steady boy,' he added, as somewhere nearby a bird chattered a warning and Nipper's ears swivelled nervously. 'Sometimes one type of plant or tree can take over, which isn't good, as animals need different types of food and different places to make their homes.

34

Cutting back something that's taking over can help other things to grow. Maybe that's what they're doing here.'

'But it's such a mess,' Grace argued. 'There's nothing for *any* animals now.'

'Look – there are lots of saplings coming through, and once the work is finished then other things will start to grow back too, I'm sure of it.'

Grace wasn't convinced. 'Do you think Grandad knows about this? His land ends right next to where they're working. Whoever did this better not start on Grandad's trees! He'll be hopping mad.'

Aaron looked around. 'It doesn't look as if they're going any further.' His gaze strayed to the river.

Grace realised he was watching a mallard peacefully glide down the middle of the current. 'Still watching out for your otters?' she teased him.

Aaron grinned. 'I can't help it!' he said.

Grace shook her head, smiling. But then something caught her eye. 'Look, there's a dead fish over there.' She pointed to a silvery fish with glassy eyes floating amongst the reeds.

'That's strange,' said Aaron. 'Otters eat what they catch. They wouldn't just leave it like that. Hey, steady there, Nipper,' he added, soothing his pony, who was beginning to fidget.

'Maybe a heron killed it?'

'It might have, but fish do just die sometimes,' said Aaron, shrugging.

'I suppose,' said Grace, losing interest. She sighed. 'We ought to turn back. I promised Gabriela that I'd pull up the weeds in the yard, and Daisy's tack needs a clean.'

They turned around, the horses picking their way back through the woods to the greenway. As they rode home, Grace found she couldn't stop thinking about the mess the woods had been left in. It was grand for Aaron to say it helped with plant growth, but what about all the creatures that had suddenly lost their homes?

As the greenway came out of the woods, the river snaked round to meet it.

'Would you look at that!' Grace exclaimed. 'Over there, by the bank. Another dead fish. Wait! There are two more, no, three. That makes *four* dead fish altogether. That's too weird. And look at the river! It's not usually this muddy. I can't see the bottom anymore.'

Aaron was watching an empty crisp packet float past. 'We should get that out. Plastic bags are the worst. An animal might try to eat it or get stuck inside it and suffocate.'

'We need a stick.' With Aaron's help, Grace searched the ground for something to hook the bag out with. By the time they found one long enough, the wrapper had floated away.

'I don't get it,' said Grace. 'The river's usually much cleaner than this.'

Aaron agreed. 'Something's not right.' His eyes widened suddenly. 'It's been polluted! *That's* why the fish are dying.'

Grace rounded on Aaron. 'What about the ponies? We let them drink from it!'

'They didn't drink much,' said Aaron. 'And the otter and her cubs were swimming in it, and they seemed OK.'

Grace's chest tightened anxiously. 'But for how long?'

'I don't know. If it's pollution, we need to know what's causing it. If something's poisoning the fish, it might not be long before it kills other, larger animals, like the otters ...' He trailed off, his face worried.

'Let's investigate!' Grace's mouth set in a firm line as she made up her mind to turn detective.

'I'm in,' said Aaron, sitting up straighter on Nipper. Daisy whickered, as if in agreement.

'Awesome,' said Grace. 'And once we work out who the culprit is, we'll make them stop what they're doing before they hurt the otters!'

Chapter 4

The scheduled lessons and rides had finished by the time Grace and Aaron returned to the stables. The teenage stable-hands, Shannon and Aleksy, were already in the yard with Star and Bonnie, waiting for Gabriela. They helped out on Saturdays and sometimes after school in exchange for free lessons. They waved at Grace and Aaron as they led their ponies past.

After walking Daisy and Nipper around long enough to cool them off, Grace and Aaron washed the mud from their ponies' legs and brushed them down. Daisy nibbled the end of Grace's plait affectionately as Grace lifted the pony's hooves to check for stones. Nipper, who wasn't so keen on being pampered, snorted impatiently, stamping a hoof as Aaron groomed him.

When the ponies were both settled in their stables, Grace went to pull up the weeds, then swept the yard before joining Aaron, who was cleaning Nipper's tack. Then it was time for the evening stables routine. Grace and Aaron came out of the hay barn with full hay nets just as the others returned from their ride, their faces glowing with happiness.

'That was great craic,' said Shannon, dismounting. She pulled off her helmet and shook out her long, strawberry-blonde hair. 'Gabriela said we could jump next week!' She patted Star's neck, and the chestnut pony whickered and rubbed her head on Shannon's arm.

'You're a natural,' Grace said. When Shannon
had started helping out at the stables a few months
ago, she'd never even sat on a horse, and now she was
learning to jump.

'Gabriela's a great teacher,' said Shannon
generously. 'Come on, Star, let's get you sorted before
Mam gets here.'

For once, everyone seemed in a hurry to get
home. Gabriela was going to Dublin for a night out

with her friends. Shannon and Aleksy were being picked up early by busy parents, and Grace and Aaron were keen to get started on researching who could be polluting the river. Grace was going to Aaron's for dinner, so, once the horses were fed and watered, they left Gabriela locking up the tack room and cycled back to his place.

Aaron's home, a bungalow on the corner of a quiet street, was a ten-minute walk from Grace's family's terraced house. He lived with his parents, his seven-year-old sister Orla and his nana. Aaron and Grace wheeled their bikes round the side of the house to the back garden. Nana opened the back door to let them in through the kitchen.

'Your mam and dad will be home soon. I baked some scones, and you can have a mineral to keep you going,' she said as they went inside.

Grace's eyes lit up. Aaron's nana was a brilliant baker. She always won a prize for her cakes at the annual Greenfort St Patrick's Day Festival.

'Thanks, Mrs Collins. Your scones are so tasty.'
Grace's stomach rumbled in agreement, and she
giggled. 'Sorry about that! I'm starving.'

'Leave some for Orla,' Nana warned as she put a
plate of freshly baked scones on the table in front of
them. 'I'll just go see where she's got to.'

Grace ate a buttered scone, savouring every
warm morsel in happy silence. Licking the last
crumbs from her fingers, she said, 'So, we need a
plan to find out who's causing the river pollution.

Let's write down everything we know. Then we can make a list of who we think might be responsible.'

'The first bit's easy,' Aaron said, taking another scone. 'We know the river's being polluted because it looked dirty and we found four dead fish.'

'We need some paper, or better still a notebook.' Grace was very organised. At school, she planned her work carefully, making lists and using coloured gel pens to highlight important facts.

Aaron grinned. 'You can have my maths workbook if you like. That's got lots of empty pages in it!'

'Won't you get a detention when your teacher finds out? Anyway, you like maths, you're good at it,' said Grace.

'I like puzzles,' Aaron corrected her. 'Nana will have paper. I'll go ask her for some.'

Aaron went to look for his nana and returned a few minutes later holding a notebook with flowers on the cover. 'She gave me this,' he said with a grimace. 'It was a birthday present, but she's never used it.'

'It's pretty.' Grace opened the book. 'What about a pencil?'

'Doh!' Aaron smacked his hand to his head. He opened a drawer behind him and rummaged through the contents before pulling out a pen. 'Any good?' he asked.

'Thanks.' In neat capital letters, Grace wrote on the first page, 'INVESTIGATION'. She underlined it, then wrote, 'Who or what is polluting the Greenwater River?' On a fresh page under the heading 'EVIDENCE' she listed their findings so far.

'Suspects?' she said, pen poised. 'Any ideas who might be responsible?'

'Meadow Farm?' suggested Aaron.

'You're kidding!' Meadow Farm was across the road from Rowan Tree Stables and its nearest neighbour. 'It's not Meadow Farm,' Grace said indignantly. 'Grandad's known Pat O'Malley practically his whole life. Pat's lovely. There's no way he'd pollute the river.'

'I'm not saying he's doing it deliberately,' said Aaron. 'But look at the evidence. He owns land on both sides of the road, doesn't he? Some of his fields run down to the river. It's been lashing down recently. If the ground can't soak up all of the rain, then it runs off the fields and into the river. If Pat puts slurry or chemicals like fertiliser on his fields, then they might end up in the river when it rains.'

'Accidental pollution, then,' said Grace thoughtfully. 'That makes more sense. OK, we'll put Meadow Farm down as our first suspect. Who else? Are there any other farms along the river? We need a map, really.'

'I'll get the laptop,' said Aaron.

It didn't take long to bring up a map of the area. They found Greenfort, then Rowan Tree Stables on the main road just outside it. Aaron used the trackpad to move the cursor along the river towards Dublin. Apart from the greenway, marked with a white line, there was little else but fields along the route.

'What's that building, there?' Grace pointed at a red location pin on the screen.

Aaron enlarged the area. 'Meath's Candles. It's quite small, but it's right on the river and there's another building a bit further on.' He moved the arrow. 'The Greenfort water-pumping plant. The candle-making business is a definite suspect, but I'm not so sure about the water plant. What do you think?'

'They're both suspects until we can rule them out,' said Grace firmly, and she wrote the two names down in the notebook.

Aaron looked thoughtful. 'We could ride over on the ponies tomorrow to check them out?'

Grace hesitated. She'd hoped to go back to the Furzebush Field to jump. Immediately, she felt guilty. What was she thinking? It was bad enough finding so many dead fish, imagine if it had been the otter family! The riding school was closed for lessons on

Sundays, so there was less to do at the stables. Then she remembered something, and her heart sank.

'We can't go tomorrow! It's the regional triathlon trials. We're competing all day.'

'Oh, flip!' said Aaron. 'I totally forgot.'

'Me too!' Grace couldn't believe it. Along with Aaron and their club mates, she'd been in training for the regional trials for ages. Now the big day had almost arrived, and she'd nearly forgotten about it! She'd packed her sports bag for it days ago, but now she couldn't get the cute little otter pups and their slinky mother off her mind.

Quietly, she asked, 'Could we miss the competition?'

Chapter 5

Aaron sighed heavily, his cheeks blowing out. 'The club's counting on us. If we win tomorrow, we qualify for the Nationals.'

For a fleeting moment, Grace thought of her teammates. It wasn't a given that she and Aaron would win, and if they dropped out it would give someone else a better chance of going through to the Nationals. But she really wanted to compete! She'd worked so hard for this opportunity. They both had, attending extra sessions at the club, practising at home and somehow managing to squeeze in pony time too. To give up their places now, after so much effort, would be hugely disappointing. Grace was lost in her thoughts when the kitchen door crashed open. Startled, she almost fell off her chair as Aaron's little sister, Orla, rushed in like a human whirlwind.

Orla ran over to her big brother and, posing dramatically, hands on hips, demanded, 'Where are the scones? There'll be trouble if you've not left me any. I'm starving!'

'Hi, Orla, the scones are right here,' said Grace, pushing the plate towards her.

Orla tossed her head, letting her long, blonde hair swish over her shoulder as she swung round to face Grace. 'Hiya. Will you play with me? I wasn't allowed to have a friend over and I'm soooo bored! Aaron's always out, and even when he is here he never wants to do anything with me.'

'Orla, stop acting the maggot,' said Aaron. 'You've got a friend coming to play tomorrow. I heard you arrange it with Mam.'

Orla ignored him and began to eat a scone, nibbling at it in small bites. When she'd finished, she started up again with the complaints. 'There's nothing to do, and I'm really bored. Grace wants to play with me, don't you, Grace? Pleeeeeeease ...' She turned beseeching eyes on her.

'Leave Grace alone,' said Aaron. 'We're busy. I'll play with you another time.'

'Busy doing what? Ooh, that's Nana's notebook,' Orla suddenly squeaked. 'Does she know you've got it?' Her hand shot out and she snatched the notebook away from Grace. 'Investigation. What does that mean? Are you writing a story?'

'Orla, stop it,' warned Aaron. 'Give us the book and go away. I've said I'll play with you another time.'

'Make me!' Orla flashed a defiant grin at Aaron and then skipped away, waving the notebook in the air.

'Orla!' Aaron chased after her. 'Give me the book. *Now!*'

Orla ran round the table giggling as she darted about, twisting and turning and changing direction to stop Aaron from catching her.

'Orla!' roared Aaron. He slid across the tiled floor, bumped into a chair and fell over, landing on his bottom.

Orla cracked up laughing. Aaron scowled, and Grace hid a chuckle as he staggered up. 'Steady!' she said, righting the chair. 'Hey, Orla, what if I plait your hair? Then will you give us the notebook and let us be?'

'Really?' said Orla, ducking out of Aaron's reach as he made another grab for her. She clutched the notebook to her chest. 'You'll plait my hair? Like now?'

'Right this very minute.' Grace loved styling hair and never went anywhere without spare clips and hair ties. She stuck her hand in her pocket and brought out a pretty hair clip decorated with a line of sparkly horseshoes. 'You can borrow my special slide until I go home.'

Giving Aaron a smug smile, Orla went to stand by Grace. 'OK,' she said. 'But I want a fishtail plait. Do you know how to do one?'

Grace raised an eyebrow. *'Do I know how?* I taught myself on Daisy!' Grace held out a hand for the notebook. Orla hesitated, but then handed it over with a cheeky grin.

'Wait there. I'm going to get my hairbrush.' Orla raced away along the hallway to her bedroom.

Grace enjoyed brushing out Orla's long, thick hair before deftly weaving it into an elaborate fishtail plait. The whole time, Orla didn't stop chattering, barely pausing for breath. Grace couldn't help admiring her spirit. Orla knew exactly what she wanted and how to get it! Aaron rolled his eyes at Grace, and she grinned. They both knew he was a big softie at heart and mighty proud of his little sister, however infuriating she was.

Grace secured Orla's hair with a red scrunchie before fixing the pretty horseshoe clip on one side. 'There. All done.'

Orla jumped up and turned in a slow circle. 'How do I look?'

'Like Cinderella ready to go to the ball,' said Nana, appearing in the doorway.

'Pah!' Orla spat. 'Who wants to look like her? What a wimp, letting herself be bossed around by her nasty sisters. Nana, can you take a picture of me on your phone?'

With the photo taken, Orla went off to watch *Ireland's Fittest Family* on television, calling out to Grace and Aaron as she skipped away, 'Good luck with the investigation!'

'Investigation?' asked Nana. 'Aaron, what's going on?'

'Nothing. It's not how it sounds.' Quickly, Aaron told his nana about their ride along the river and what they'd discovered.

'We want to find out who's responsible,' he finished.

'We were going to investigate it tomorrow,' Grace added. Encouraged by the attentive way Aaron's nana was listening, she went on, 'There's a company that makes candles and a water-pumping station next to the river. Either might be causing the pollution. Only, we've just remembered it's the triathlon trials, and ...' She paused, unsure how to continue.

Nana looked from Grace to Aaron. 'It's the Regionals, isn't it? The winners go through to compete in the Nationals. You surely can't be thinking about pulling out of that over a few dead fish? It wouldn't be right. The club has invested time and money in you. All those extra training sessions you've had. Not everyone gets those.'

There was an awkward silence. Grace felt her face flush with embarrassment. Nana had a point. They'd put themselves forward for the competition, and they'd been chosen to compete on merit. Only a handful of children from each age group had been picked. They were the club's hopefuls, the ones that stood a chance of winning medals. To pull out now wouldn't just be wrong, it would be poor sportsmanship. Grace was filled with shame.

'No, of course not,' she said, and to her relief Aaron agreed.

Nana's smile made her blue eyes twinkle kindly. 'I'm not surprised the river seemed dirty. It's rained nonstop this week. The extra water will have stirred up mud from the riverbed.

59

Give it a few days, and the water will be running clear again, I'm sure. The fish and the otters will be fine. You'll see.' She patted Aaron on the arm. 'Now, how about I start some dinner? Your mam and dad will be here any minute.'

'You're probably right. Thanks, Nana,' said Aaron, even though he didn't look completely convinced.

Grace wasn't either, but there was nothing more they could do until after the triathlon event.

She really hoped the otters would be OK.

Chapter 6

Grace woke early the next morning, still thinking about the otters. She forced her concerns away. She had to focus on the triathlon, in particular the swimming, her weakest sport. Nervously, she checked her bag for the umpteenth time to make sure she'd packed her togs, swimming cap and towel. Grace loved to swim but mostly for fun. She was looking forward to getting it over and done with so that she could enjoy the cycling and then the run. She ate a light breakfast and then sat sipping a glass of fruit juice.

'Grace, it's time to go.' Mam chivvied her into the car but not before Grace had double-checked that her bike was securely fastened to the rack at the back.

They arrived in the car park at the same time as Aaron and his dad.

'Are you leaving home?' Grace teased, prodding Aaron's bulging sports bag. 'What's in there?'

Sheepishly, Aaron grinned back at her. 'What haven't I got in there! I keep meaning to empty it out, but there's never time.'

Grace patted her own neatly packed bag. She always made a list so as not to forget anything. 'Did you remember your togs this time?'

'I'm wearing them!' said Aaron. He lowered his voice. 'I've brought a book on wildlife with me. I reread the chapter on pollution last night. I thought we could have a look at it together over lunch.'

Mam unhitched Grace's bike and left, promising to return in time for the races and bring Grace's big brother, Finn. Aaron's dad was also returning with Aaron's mam but not his nana, who'd opted to stay home and look after Orla and her friend.

Grace and Aaron went straight to their respective changing rooms before the visiting teams arrived. It only took Grace a moment to change into her togs, pulling on her Greenfort Triathlon Club shorts, t-shirt and hoodie.

She went and joined her teammates in the club hall for the ritual touching of the silver shamrock. The shamrock was usually kept in a locked glass case. It was the first trophy the club had won over twenty years ago when the club was founded. From then on, it had been the tradition for anyone competing in an event to touch the silver shamrock for luck.

Grace hovered at the back of the hall, watching out for Aaron and lining up with him to touch the shamrock together – their own lucky tradition! Afterwards, they went outside to watch as the other clubs started to arrive until it was time to register and collect their numbers.

Grace was about to line up for hers when Clodagh, her best friend from school, arrived.

'Late as usual!' said Grace, hanging back to wait for her as she did a quick change.

Clodagh grinned. 'Why waste good sleeping time?'

The girls would be competing first, so Grace and Clodagh left Aaron with a group of his friends, picked up their numbers and headed over to the under-11s girls' warm-up session, run by Grace's favourite coach, a sporty young woman called Ella.

Although the late spring day was chilly, with a biting wind, Grace was lovely and warm by the time she lined up with Clodagh and the other girls on the banks of the river. She couldn't help peering suspiciously into the water as she tucked her hair into an orange swim cap.

'It's fine,' said Aaron, appearing at her side. 'I checked it earlier. The pollution doesn't seem to have

reached this far. Good luck!' he added, giving her a
high-five.

'Thanks!' Grace replied, discarding her towel.

Grace waited for the whistle and then dived into
the icy water. Initially paralysed with shock at the cold,
once she got her breath back, she went on to swim her
best time and came in a healthy third. Clodagh was
also happy with her tenth-place finish. Back on dry
land and wrapped up in huge, fluffy towels, Grace and
Clodagh hung around to watch Aaron swim.

Aaron was strong in the water. He and another
Greenfort boy called Jack led the pack all the way.
As they approached the finish, Grace screamed at the
top of her lungs, cheering Aaron home. He came first,
half a stroke ahead of Jack.

'It was my cheering that made you win,' Grace told him as he staggered out of the freezing water.

'Course it was. Nothing to do with my overall brilliance and fitness!' Aaron quipped back.

The cycling was next. Grace looked over enviously at the girls from the Templeton Club, who were all riding very expensive bikes. Next to them, the Castlekenny girls were doing a weird kind of bonding jig, pulling faces at the opposing teams before they mounted their bikes. They didn't scare Grace, though. Cycling to and from the stables every day had helped her fitness a lot. When the race started, she paced herself, cycling at the front but not in the lead until the home stretch, when she embraced her inner racehorse. Head down, legs pumping, she crossed the winning line first, to the disbelief of the Templeton girl who'd led the whole way round. Clodagh came in ninth and was happy with her time. Then it was Aaron's turn. He came in third, missing second place by a microsecond. He said he was more annoyed than disappointed, reminding Grace just how competitive they both were when it came to events!

There was a break for lunch next but no time to look at Aaron's book, as the three families all sat together having a spontaneous picnic. Munching on a sandwich, Grace stared round at all the competitors scattered around the field and sighed happily. Competition days were fun. She was glad they had come after all. Grace finished eating and then went with Aaron and Clodagh to ask their coach if they could help with anything while they waited for their last event.

'It would be nice for you guys to cheer on our other teams in their races,' said Ella, so they did, shouting loudly for the girls and boys competing in the under-13s and the under-15s cycling races.

At last, it was time for their final event, the run. Grace nervously fumbled with her laces as she put on her runners. Only two competitors from each age group went forward to compete at the Nationals.

Grace had checked the scoreboard and knew she had to win the running to secure her place.

'Focus!' she told herself, pushing all thoughts of polluted rivers and otters out of her head as she lined up with the other competitors. When the starting pistol fired, Grace sprinted off, tailing a tall girl running for Templeton who'd taken an early lead. No matter how hard the girl tried to pull away, Grace kept with her, finally coming alongside as they reached the home stretch. The spectators went wild. Spurred on by the roaring crowd, Grace inched ahead and finished first, beating her Templeton rival by the length of her trainer. Grace punched the air, knowing her place at the Nationals was secure. She smiled with relief before being enveloped in a big hug by her mam and her big brother Finn. Aaron ran over to congratulate her too, followed closely by their coach.

'Well done. I'm so proud of you,' said Ella. 'You really deserve this win.' She carried on

talking about Grace's talent, hard work and overall commitment to the sport as Grace squirmed inside, grateful that her coach didn't know how close she'd come to mitching!

Grace couldn't fully bask in her own victory until she knew that Aaron was going to the Nationals with her. She needn't have worried, though. Aaron was on fire in his race. She'd never seen him so focused. He threw himself over the finishing line, winning with a clear lead. Grace clapped him on the back when she finally made it through a cheering crowd of boys to congratulate him. 'Well done!'

The two of them hung around for the prize-giving, watching the other age groups finish competing while they waited. The ceremony went on for ages. The younger competitors were given their medals first. Grace and Aaron received shields for winning the Regionals and medals for each of the events they'd been placed in or won.

Then they had to sit very still so as not to clink and disturb the prize-giving as the older competitors collected their medals. But, at last, it was over.

'See you tomorrow,' said Aaron, climbing into the back of his dad's car.

'Meet by the Greenfort library after school, and don't be late,' called Grace.

Aaron grinned. 'Who, me?'

'I'm not waiting for you!' Grace shouted as the car pulled slowly away.

They both knew she would. Aaron gave her a thumbs up, and Grace grinned back, shaking her head. She could hardly wait. Tomorrow, after school, they'd finally be able to ride the ponies along the greenway to investigate Meath's Candles.

That evening, Grace planned the ride in her head as she soaked in a warm bath with a large dollop of her mother's special cherry bubble bath. She'd whipped the bubbles into a tower of froth so only her nose was visible. Clean water was something Grace took for granted. She'd never really thought how lucky she was to have it. It made her all the more determined to help the otters and all the other wildlife living on or around the river. In her mind, Grace had already decided that Meath's Candles was the culprit. Tomorrow, they would gather all the evidence they needed to get the factory to stop whatever it was they were doing wrong. After that, they would force the business to clean up the river. Then she and Aaron could finally stop worrying about it.

Chapter 7

To Grace's surprise, Aaron beat her to the library the following afternoon. She found him already waiting outside, sitting on his bike with his feet on the ground, reading the wildlife book.

'I was just about to leave without you,' he teased as she pulled up next to him.

'See you emptied your bag then,' said Grace.

She smiled as Aaron tried to ram the book back inside his still-bulging bag.

They cycled to the stables in a record eight minutes, screeching into the yard seconds before the arrival of the first cars bringing the children for Gabriela's Tack and Hack club. The after-school club, held once a week on a Monday, gave children the opportunity to ride and care for a pony for two hours, and it was very popular.

Aaron and Grace hovered in the pony barn, watching over the young riders as they tacked up.

'Need some help there?' asked Grace, slipping inside the stable where a small girl called Emilia was struggling to get a bridle on a Shetland called Cinders.

'Cinders keeps shaking her head,' said Emilia.

'Pack it in,' Grace told the little pony firmly. She stood by Cinders' shaggy, brown head, holding onto the headcollar, which was now round the pony's neck.

'Thank you!' Emilia gave Grace a huge grin, revealing a gap where she'd lost a tooth. Her fingers fumbled with the bridle, and Grace watched patiently, resisting the urge to do up the buckle for her.

'Well done,' Grace said when the bridle was finally secure. 'Now, are you riding bareback?'

'No! I'd fall off!' Emilia had a fit of the giggles, and then suddenly her eyes widened. 'Oh! I get it. I forgot to collect my saddle.'

'Go on, so,' prompted Grace. 'I'll hold Cinders for you.'

At last, the ride was ready to leave. Gabriela swung herself up into Merlin's saddle. 'Ready, everyone? Any problems, just shout. *Vamos!* Let's go!'

Gabriela walked Merlin through the gate and into the field, before looking back to check that her group was following. Grace held her breath as she watched to see which way they'd ride along the greenway. She hoped it was in the opposite direction from Meath's Candles. Gabriela wouldn't be too pleased if they distracted the other horses by overtaking them, and Grace didn't want to have to explain their investigation before they'd made any real progress.

Gabriela and Merlin reached the track and swung right towards Greenfort, with the Tack and Hack riders following in single file.

Grace's breath rushed out in relief. 'Ready?' she asked Aaron.

'Are you off riding now? Only, I made an apple cake yesterday,' said Alesky, coming into the yard. 'It's in a tin in the tack room.'

'Yummy!' said Grace. The teenage stable-hand often brought his home-made cakes and biscuits to the stables for everyone to share. His parents were from Poland, although he'd been born in Ireland, and his Polish apple cake, made with cinnamon and raisins, was the best that Grace had ever tasted. 'Thanks, Aleksy. Can we take some with us?'

'Sure! Help yourself.'

She and Aaron swiped a slice of cake each, eating it as they collected their tack.

Daisy whickered eagerly as Grace approached, impatiently stamping a hoof when Grace put the saddle on the door before opening it. The pony stretched out her neck, nostrils flaring, as she tried to work out what Grace had been eating.

'All gone,' Grace giggled as Daisy's lips tickled her palm. 'I got you an apple.' Grace pulled one from her jacket pocket and bit into it before showing Daisy the other side. Daisy's bite was much bigger than Grace's. She finished her half of the apple in two chews. Feeling full of cake, Grace fed her the rest of the apple. Then she tacked up quickly, leading Daisy out of the stable at the exact same time as Aaron and Nipper.

'He's keen to be off,' said Aaron as Nipper pranced about in the yard.

'We didn't ride yesterday, so they probably had a lazy day in the field,' Grace pointed out. She mounted Daisy.

'What's Rocky got there?' said Aaron as the Jack Russell terrier ran across his path.

Grace chuckled. 'It looks like a sock.'

'It looks like *my* sports sock. Rocky, come here!'

Rocky stopped and looked at Aaron, his head cocked. The long, green sock hanging from his mouth made him look like he had droopy whiskers. He stamped his paws, inviting Aaron to play with him.

'Rocky! You scamp. He's been through my bag,' said Aaron.

Grace laughed. 'You know what he's like. Why didn't you zip it up?'

'Rocky, drop,' said Aaron. Rocky took a step closer but then doubled back, haring off towards the tack room.

'We haven't got time to chase him,' said Grace. 'We'll have to get your sock later, c'mon, let's go.'

They trotted across the fields until they reached the greenway, then cantered parallel to it until they entered the woods. 'That was fun!' Grace patted Daisy's shoulder, bringing her back to a trot as they joined the official path.

There was no one else about, so they trotted briskly along the greenway, getting occasional glimpses of the river through the trees as they went.

'The water looks even muddier today,' said Aaron, frowning.

They rode closer.

'There are more dead fish, over there by that tree with its roots in the water.' Grace spotted five lifeless fish caught between the roots of a tree clinging to the edge of the bank. She urged Daisy on, suddenly scared for the otter family. *What would they find when they reached their holt?*

*

'No otters.' Aaron sounded disappointed. He halted Nipper and stared longingly across the river at the bush masking the otter's den.

'No sick otters either,' said Grace, trying to be positive. The river was even dirtier here, a gunky brown with scum on the surface. Grace counted six more dead fish, one with savage bites taken out of it. Her stomach turned and she looked away. What had been eating the poisoned fish? She hoped it wasn't the otters.

They rode on, past the tree-clearing operation where four workers in high-vis jackets were busy stacking logs. The cleared ground was barren, and, even though Aaron kept insisting that thinning the trees and overgrowth would likely benefit the area, Grace wasn't convinced. It looked sad and empty to her.

A while later, they reached Meath's Candles. It was closer to the stables than it had looked on the map, and the building was smaller than Grace had expected.

'I think we can rule out Meath's Candles,' Aaron said almost immediately. 'The building's too far from the river, and, unless there's an underground pipe somewhere, the factory isn't discharging anything into the water.'

'You're right,' said Grace. 'You can tell from the river. It's very clear here, and there aren't any dead fish.' She checked her watch. 'Shall we ride on? We can get to the water-pumping station if we're quick.'

'If the pollution is further upstream, then we'd see evidence of it here, surely?' said Aaron.

'Good point,' agreed Grace. 'But since we've come this far, let's check it out anyway.'

Grace was enjoying the ride too much to turn back. She asked Daisy to trot on, savouring the warmth of the sun and the fresh breeze on her face as she rose up and down in time with Daisy's comfortable gait.

All too soon, they reached the water-pumping station. The one-storey building looked well maintained, and the grounds around it were neat and tidy. There was even a tiny car park with tubs of brightly coloured flowers along one side. Grace and Aaron inspected the river, and Aaron nodded approvingly.

'The water here is perfect. Look.' A moorhen and two mallards were peacefully floating downstream with the current.

'The ducks look happy,' said Grace. She shortened Daisy's reins to stop her from pulling towards the lush green grass growing between the greenway and the river.

'Looks like we've managed to rule out two of our suspects,' said Aaron as they turned the ponies back. 'But if it's not Meath's Candles, and it's not the pumping station, that means it has to be Meadow Farm, doesn't it?'

'It looks that way,' said Grace quietly.

Chapter 8

There was a heavy lump in Grace's stomach, like she'd accidently swallowed a rock. She couldn't bear to think that her grandad's friendly neighbour was behind the pollution. 'Pat O'Malley's sound. I'm sure he wouldn't pollute the river on purpose. Maybe he doesn't realise that it's happened.'

Aaron looked doubtful, but to Grace's relief he didn't argue with her. Changing the subject, he said, 'If we tell your grandad, do you think he'd say something to Pat for us? It might be better coming from another grown-up.'

Grace hesitated. She wasn't keen on having to tell Grandad's neighbour that he was harming the river, but at the same time she didn't want to tell Grandad either. Grandad and Pat's friendship went way back. They looked out for each other. Gabriela was renting Pat's self-contained annexe attached to his farmhouse. He had offered up the accommodation as soon as he'd heard that Grandad had a trainee instructor coming over from Spain who needed somewhere to live. He'd been very generous with the rate too. Grandad said that Pat could have made a lot more money renting the annexe to holiday-makers.

Suddenly Grace wished they hadn't started the investigation. Maybe they should just keep quiet about their findings and wait for someone else to notice that the river was being polluted? *No!* Grace knew she was being a coward. So many fish had died already. What next, if they kept quiet – the ducks, the otters? Grace remembered the otter pups splashing around in the water and her chest tightened.

'I think we should tell Grandad what we've found when we get back. He might offer to talk to Pat for us.' *With any luck*, thought Grace, crossing her fingers.

*

When they rode back into the yard, it was full of ponies and children. The Tack and Hack club had just returned, and Gabriela stood in the middle of the group instructing the children on how to look after their ponies now the ride was over.

Grace and Aaron took Daisy and Nipper back to their stables and made them comfortable. Grace was just hanging up Daisy's bridle in the tack room when she felt someone tug at her sleeve. She turned to find Emilia trying to get her attention.

'Bonnie's loose in the pony barn,' Emilia lisped.

'How did that happen?' Grace exclaimed.

'Ollie forgot to do the kick bolt and Bonnie escaped. You're not cross, are you? Ollie said to come and get you because you're never cross.'

Emilia's honesty made Grace chuckle. 'I'm not cross, just confused. Ollie wasn't riding Bonnie.'

'Gabriela told us to give our ponies a hay net. Bonnie started kicking her door because she wanted one too. Ollie went and filled Bonnie's hay net, but he forgot about the kick bolt, and when he came back Bonnie had escaped.' Emilia stared up at Grace with huge, green eyes.

Grace grinned. 'That sounds like Bonnie. Come on, then. Let's go catch her.' Grace grabbed a headcollar and raced to the pony barn where Ollie and another small boy were unsuccessfully trying to herd Bonnie back into her stable.

With the help of a packet of mints, Bonnie came straight to Grace.

'Bonnie, you bold girl,' said Grace, stroking the pony's face as she munched on a mint. Bonnie whinnied and tried to stick her nose in Grace's pocket as she put the mints away.

'Greedy guts,' said Grace fondly, rubbing the pony's nose. She fed Bonnie another mint, checked that her hay net was secure and left the stable, bolting the door both at the top and the bottom. As Grace spun round, she almost tripped over Emilia, who was right behind her. Emilia gave her a big hug before skipping off to the yard to wait for her mam.

Grandad was also in the yard, greeting parents as they collected their children. Rocky was lying in a patch of evening sunshine, stretched out on his side. He rolled onto his back, his paws pedalling the air and his tail swishing back and forth, inviting Grace to rub his tummy as she approached. Grace obliged but not for long, as it was time for the evening stables routine.

Grace and Aaron were the only helpers left. Shannon and Aleksy had gone home after the Tack and Hack club finished, but she and Aaron worked fast, and it wasn't long before the horses were settled for the night. Grandad sent Gabriela home next, saying he'd do the final walk around and lock up.

Grace and Aaron hung around outside the tack room waiting for him to finish. Grace picked up the hurley and sliotar that Grandad always left propped against the pony barn.

'Fetch!' she told Rocky, hurling the sliotar across the yard.

Rocky was gone even before Grace had whacked the ball, jumping up and catching it as it sailed above his head and racing back to Grace. He dropped the ball at her feet, his tail wagging like a metronome.

'Oi, Rocky, where's my sock?' Aaron asked.

Rocky went down on his front paws, bowing to Aaron, his tail wagging playfully. 'Fetch my sock,' said Aaron, pointing away from him. Rocky jumped up and ran in the direction of Aaron's arm until he realised that there was no ball to chase. He came back, throwing himself down at Aaron's feet again with a disappointed grunt.

'Haven't you two got homes to go to?' said Grandad, coming over to lock up the tack room.

Grace and Aaron exchanged an uncomfortable look. 'Can we talk to you?' Grace asked.

'This sounds serious. What've you done?'

'Nothing,' said Aaron, hastily. 'It's about the river.'

Between them, Grace and Aaron told Grandad about the pollution and their concerns for the fish, otters and other wildlife. Grandad listened attentively, sometimes interrupting to ask them to repeat a point. Then Grace took a deep breath and, in a rush, explained their fears that Meadow Farm was responsible.

'No,' said Grandad decisively. 'Not a chance! Pat knows all about the problems of run-off, he'd know if rainwater was washing fertiliser into the river. Besides, he doesn't use chemicals on his land. He's an environmentalist first, farmer second, always has been.'

'But if it isn't him, then who is it?' said Grace. She could see from the set of Aaron's jaw that he wasn't convinced either.

'No idea,' said Grandad gruffly. 'It's too late to ride out now, but I'll try to take a look tomorrow when I'm exercising Storm. And in the meantime, you two are *not* to go spreading rumours about Pat or anyone else. You need evidence before you start making accusations like that.'

Grace and Aaron nodded.

Grandad put his arm around Grace and pulled her in for a hug. 'I know you meant well, and it's grand that you both care so much about the environment. We've only got one planet!'

Leaving the hurley and sliotar against the barn, Grace and Aaron said goodbye to Grandad. 'What now?' Grace asked, once they were out of her grandad's earshot. 'I don't want Meadow Farm to be responsible, but there isn't anyone else, is there?'

Aaron was equally baffled. 'We must be missing something, but what?'

Grace sighed. She really wanted them to solve the mystery of the polluted river, but it was more important to get the polluter stopped quickly. If that meant Grandad solving it, then she could live with that. 'Grandad will work it out,' she said, confidently.

Chapter 9

The following day, Grace raced home from school. 'Can I ring Grandad?' she shouted as she burst through the door. Oscar, the family's chocolate brown Labrador, ambled along the hall to greet her, his tail wagging amicably.

'Hello, boy, did you miss me?' Grace knelt down to pat him, laughing as Oscar licked her face and hands.

'Hello,' Mam called out from the kitchen.
'I missed you too. Did you have a good day?'

'Hi, Mam.' Grace dumped her school bag by
the stairs before going to give her mam a swift hug.
'School was OK. Please can I ring Grandad?'

'He rang you already,' said Finn. Grace's brother
backed out of the fridge with a mineral and a block of
cheese. 'He left a message and said not to worry about
calling him back.'

'What was the message?' Grace was bursting to know if Grandad had discovered who was polluting the river.

Finn put the cheese on a board and rummaged in the drawer for a knife. 'Hmmmm, what did he say now? Let me think. Does anyone want a slice of cheese?'

'Finn, stop messing with me!' Grace squealed.

'I almost had it then, but you made me forget again,' Finn said with a perfectly straight face. 'Are you sure you don't want something to eat? You're going to triathlon club, aren't you? You should go and get your stuff. You're going to be late.'

'Don't tell me what to do. You're not my dad,' said Grace. Finn was even bossier now Dad and his new partner had moved to Scotland. 'Mam, make him tell me what Grandad said.'

Finn's lips twitched.

'Finn!' said Mam warningly. 'If Grandad asked you to pass a message on to Grace, then please give it to her.'

Carefully, Finn lined up the blade of the knife and cut a slice of cheese. 'Not much to tell,' he said. 'Just something about there being lots of dead fish in the river and that he was looking into it. Oh, and he said not to worry about the otters because he found fresh spraints.'

'Spraints?' Grace asked.

'Poo,' said Finn. 'Did you see an otter, then? And what's all this about dead fish?'

Tempting as it was to annoy Finn and tease him back, Grace didn't have time. Quickly, she told Mam and Finn everything, from discovering that the river was being polluted, to her and Aaron's fears for the otter family. Mam seemed shocked, saying pollution had never been a problem in the area before.

'Well done for letting your grandad know,' she said. 'He's the man to get to the bottom of it. Now, away with you or you'll be late for triathlon.'

Grace ran upstairs to her bedroom and swapped her school bag for her sports bag. Unlike Aaron, who had one bag for everything, organised Grace liked to keep her home and school life separate.

*

Grace's mind was on the otters as she cycled to triathlon club. What was Grandad looking into? Had he found out something that he wasn't letting on about? Grace was desperate to know more. She arrived at the club hall just as Aaron was padlocking his bike to the fence. 'Aaron,' she called. Braking alongside him, she lowered her voice. 'Wanna mitch club?'

'What?' Aaron stood up quickly. 'Why? What's happened?'

'Nothing yet. Grandad phoned. He's looking into the river pollution, whatever than means! Shall we go and help him?'

'So, you want to mitch off club?'

'It won't matter if we miss a week,' said Grace. 'We deserve a rest after the competition.'

Aaron frowned. 'But Ella said that we'd be starting training for the Nationals today. Competition's going to be much stronger than it was for the Regionals. We'll be up against the best in Ireland. If Denis is looking into it, then we should probably leave it to him?'

'It might take him ages, and what about the otters? What if they can't survive that long in the polluted water? Besides, we spend hours training by ourselves. We can easily do extra at home to make up for it,' Grace added persuasively. She held her breath, willing Aaron to agree with her.

For a few agonising seconds he said nothing, but at last he nodded. 'Sure. We'll go to the stables then, but I can't be late home. If I'm not back when club finishes, then Mam will know something's up.'

Grace felt suddenly very uncomfortable. She hadn't thought about what she'd tell her mam. The truth, she guessed, in case Grandad mentioned that they'd been at the stables. She hadn't thought that Aaron would have to lie to his parents. 'Are you sure you're OK about coming with me?' she asked.

'Yes,' said Aaron, 'I'm sure.'

They cycled to the stables and went to collect their tack. Grace was surprised to find Daisy's bridle and saddle were missing. Someone must be riding her pony. She checked the list of rides on the wall. Daisy was down for a private lesson at four o'clock. Grace frowned. It wasn't as if Daisy was needed. She scanned the list again. There were plenty of other suitable ponies not being used in the group lesson that was running at the same time.

Aaron was reading the list over Grace's shoulder. 'Daisy's being used, so you can ride Nipper and I'll ride my bike.' He offered up Nipper's bridle and saddle to her.

'Thanks, but no.' Grace felt suddenly upset. What was the point of having your own pony if you couldn't ride her when you wanted to? She headed for the pony barn. Gabriela was in Daisy's stable, tacking her up. Daisy whickered a greeting to Grace.

'Stand still,' Gabriela said. She looked up, surprise then confusion flashing across her face. '*Hola*, Grace, I thought you had triathlon club on a Tuesday?'

'I do, usually,' said Grace. 'But today I wanted to ride Daisy instead.'

Gabriela nodded sympathetically. '*Sí*, I understand. I often feel like that. When you want to ride and you have a pony, then nothing can stop you. Luckily for you, *señorita*, Daisy will be free shortly. I'm taking a private lesson. It's only for half an hour. Shall I leave Daisy tacked up for you?'

Gabriela was being very reasonable, but Grace, blinded by guilt for persuading Aaron to skip triathlon and fearful for the otters, felt cross and disappointed. She scowled at Gabriela. 'Why do you have to use Daisy? Primrose and Star are both free.'

'Primrose has already been ridden twice today, and my client isn't up to Star.'

Grace opened her mouth to argue. But just then Grandad appeared from Bear's stable.

'Hiya, Grace, I thought I heard you. What's occurring? Why aren't you at triathlon?'

'I felt like riding instead,' said Grace grumpily. 'I didn't realise it would be such a problem.'

Grandad looked at her for a long moment, and Grace felt herself blush. 'There are plenty of ponies available to ride immediately, but not Daisy. You don't usually come by on a Tuesday evening. Has triathlon club been cancelled?'

Grace squirmed and stared at her feet, unable to look at her grandad. 'Club's still on, but we wanted to ride out and check on the otters. We can't stop thinking about what will happen to them if we don't find out who's polluting the river.'

'I said I'd look into it. Did you let your coaches know that you wouldn't be at club today? Did you ask your mam?'

'Um, I ... No, it was a spur of the moment kind of a thing,' Grace mumbled.

Grandad shook his head. 'Then I'm sorry, my lovely, but I can't possibly let you ride. It wouldn't be fair. You won a place in the Nationals. Opportunities like that don't come along every day. You owe it to your club, your teammates and yourself to give it your best shot. And another thing, your mam thinks you're at triathlon club. Imagine if something had happened to you on the way here! How would she know? It might have been ages before anyone realised that you were missing and came looking for you.'

Grace was flooded with shame and regret. Not only had she been thoughtless, but she'd persuaded

Aaron to mitch with her. And now she'd been grouchy with Gabriela too. A lump formed in her throat, and she couldn't speak. She rammed her hands in her pockets and nodded mutely.

Grandad pulled out his mobile and checked the time. 'If you get going now, there's still time to make it back to club. Aaron, I see you there too. Leave Nipper's tack on the saddle horse, I'll put it away for you.'

'Thanks a million, Denis.' Dumping Nipper's saddle and bridle down, Aaron scuttled out of the pony barn looking embarrassed. Grace threw herself at Grandad and hugged him tightly, burying her nose in his soft jacket.

His familiar smell of horse and dog, mingled with traces of the washing powder Granny used, was deeply comforting. Grace mumbled into his chest, 'Sorry, Grandad, I messed up.'

Grandad ruffled her hair. 'You're not the first, and you won't be the last! The important thing is to know how to make it right. Now, be off with you before I start confessing all the mistakes I've made over the years!'

Chapter 10

'I still think it must be Meadow Farm causing the problem,' said Aaron the next afternoon as he paused from sweeping the stableyard to lean on his broom.

It had rained for most of the day, and when they'd arrived at the stables after school the yard had been a soggy mess. Grace, who liked things to be tidy, had decided to sweep it immediately, before the next lesson started.

'Grandad doesn't think so.' Grace shovelled up a heap of muddy straw and carried it over to the muck heap. She wasn't sure she agreed with him. While she didn't want Meadow Farm to be the ones polluting the river, there just weren't any other suspects. Sighing, she added, 'We're done here. Let's go for a ride.'

They put the brooms and shovels away and collected tack for their ponies. Nipper let out an excited snort as Aaron approached his stable. Daisy kicked her door, then pushed her nose at Grace looking for treats.

'There must be a way to test for run-off,' Grace called to Aaron as she tacked Daisy up.

'I looked on the internet,' said Aaron. 'There's something called a risk assessment that farmers can do to work out if run-off will be a problem. But the important thing is to know what's being put on the land. Your grandad said that Meadow Farm doesn't use chemicals, but does he know that for sure?'

'What if we collected a water sample from the river, either alongside Meadow Farm's fields or downstream of them?' Grace asked. She led Daisy out of the stable and into the yard. Aaron followed with Nipper.

'Good plan, but how are we going to test it? We're not chemists.'

Grace shrugged. 'There must be someone who could test it for us. What about one of the wildlife charities?' She mounted Daisy and moved away from the mounting block for Aaron.

Aaron put his foot in the stirrup, then stopped and stared at Grace. 'That's genius! We could ask the Irish Wildlife Trust. They came to our school last term and gave a talk. It was really interesting. I bet they could test a water sample for chemicals.'

'Let's do it,' said Grace. Her mind ran on ahead. It shouldn't take long to get a sample of river water. And afterwards they could ride to the Furzebush Field and do some jumping. 'We need a bottle to put the sample in, though.'

'I've got one,' said Aaron. 'Here, hold on to Nipper for me.'

Nipper let out a shrill whinny as Aaron jumped down from the mounting block and bolted across the yard. A short while later he was back, carrying a reusable water bottle.

Grace watched as Aaron attached the bottle to the D-shaped metal ring on Nipper's saddle and then hopped up onto his pony's back.

'Ready?'

Aaron nodded, and the two of them headed across the field to the greenway at the bottom.

Grace relaxed as they rode across the field towards the greenway. At last, they were off. She couldn't wait to find out who or what was polluting the river. Then she and Aaron could stop worrying about the gorgeous otters and concentrate on riding out and having fun with their ponies.

'Where shall we get the sample from?' she asked.

Aaron thought about it. 'The best place would be where all the dead fish are,' he said eventually.

They trotted along the greenway, keeping a close eye on the river. Daisy tossed her head, eager to canter, and Nipper shied away from her.

'Steady, boy,' Aaron patted his neck. 'He's not used to having a bottle bumping against him.'

The greenway swung closer to the river, and Grace said suddenly, 'The water's much dirtier here.'

'Who owns that land on the other side of the river?' Aaron asked, waving at the field opposite. It sloped down to the riverbank and had hedges growing around three sides. 'If it rains heavily, the water would run straight into the river. It might be *that* field that's causing the problem!'

'I'm not sure who owns it,' Grace said slowly. 'I think it might be part of Meadow Farm too.'

'There's a dead fish,' said Aaron.

The fish was on the bank, its body twisted, its tail trailing in the water.

'And there are more.' Further along the bank, several lifeless fish were floating in the water. There were too many to count. Grace felt sick. The problem was getting worse. Time was running out for the otters. 'Let's take our sample here,' she said.

'I think we should ride on a bit first and see if we can work out where the pollution starts,' said Aaron.

Grace agreed, and, as they continued along the greenway, she and Aaron were shocked to see how bad the pollution had become since they'd last ridden this way. 'So many dead fish,' said Grace, her nose wrinkling. 'They're beginning to smell.'

'Look at all the silt,' said Aaron.

It had rained so heavily that the water had broken the bank in places, leaving sticky, black piles of mud as it receded. They passed the bush that hid the otter holt, and Grace almost couldn't bear to look, fearing the worst.

'Phew!' said Aaron, having had a look around. 'No sign of them. I wasn't sure what we might find, but no otter has to be better than a sick one or worse.'

'Should we take a sample of the water from here?' asked Grace.

'Let's ride on a little bit further,' said Aaron.

They hadn't gone far when Grace pulled up. 'What's that?' she said, nodding at a scummy slick of broken branches, leaves and food wrappers drifting down the middle of the waterway.

Aaron asked Nipper to stop. He stared at the river for a long time before suddenly he seemed to realise something. 'It's come from the tree felling! They're contaminating the water with their rubbish. Grace, that's it! The workers felling the trees are the ones polluting it!'

'Are you sure?' Grace wanted Aaron to be right so they could put Pat O'Malley in the clear. 'They've made a mess, but is that enough to kill so many fish?'

'I'm certain,' Aaron warmed to his theory. 'I think soil's getting into the water as the contractors clear the trees growing along the riverbank. It's silting the river up and making it cloudy. I think that's why the water quality is so bad. The fish aren't getting enough oxygen from the water, so they die.'

'That's awful!' said Grace. 'Poor little fishes.'

Aaron grew more animated. 'I can't believe how long it's taken me to work it out. The evidence was right under our noses! The people working in the woods must be causing the pollution. The water was fine until they showed up, and there was never any litter before either.'

'Aaron, you're a genius!' said Grace. 'We don't need a water sample now. Let's go and tell them what's happening and ask them to stop. Then, once the silt settles, the fish will stop dying and everything will be fine again.'

Aaron turned pink. 'I'm not a genius. I should have worked it out earlier.'

'Sure, but you worked it out in the end. Come on. Let's go and sort this out.'

Chapter 11

At a fast pace, Grace and Aaron trotted along the greenway. When the path moved away from the river again, they came off it and rode through the woods, weaving their way towards the area that was being cleared. The sudden whine of a chainsaw startled both ponies. Daisy's ears swivelled, and Nipper shied and bucked. Aaron sat deep in the saddle, keeping his hands down as he gently checked the pony and tried not to fall off.

'Steady, boy,' he said calmly, stroking Nipper's neck as the pony jogged on the spot. Gradually, Nipper settled, his ears swivelling occasionally when the pitch of the chainsaw changed, getting higher as it attacked the wood.

They rode on until Grace spotted three men, dressed in fluorescent high-vis jackets and blue safety helmets, working in the clearing. A fourth person was driving a small tractor with a crane-like attachment. It was being used to load a lorry with the tree trunks.

Grace gasped. 'Look at the mess!' The churned-up ground was shocking enough, but the massacred trees and bushes were much worse, and there was so much litter. Some of it was industrial waste – cable ties, plastic wrap, cardboard, screws and nails – and some of it was food containers like bottles and cans. It was clear that the workers were treating the woods as one giant rubbish bin.

Aaron rode over to the river's edge to inspect the bank.

'It's a mess,' he called back. 'It used to be grass here, but now it's pure mud – and look at all the tyre marks.'

Grace looked round as the chainsaw stopped abruptly. Her stomach fluttered like it had suddenly grown wings. 'Someone's coming over!'

A tall man with dark, curly hair and a wind-tanned face strode towards them. The man with the chainsaw came with him.

'Well, hello there, kids,' the tall man called out. 'Have you lost your way?'

'We're not lost,' said Grace. 'We wanted to see you.'

'What's this about, then?' As the man came closer, the rest of the workers joined him, gathering around. They were much younger than Grace had first thought – even the tall one who seemed to be in charge. She eyed the chainsaw man nervously. He hadn't put the tool down and was brandishing it like a sword. It didn't look very safe. When Dad used a chainsaw to cut the garden hedge, he was really careful with it. He always pointed the blade towards the ground when he moved it.

Clearing his throat, Aaron spoke up. 'It's about the river. The work that you're doing here is putting silt into it.'

'Is that so?'

'Er, yes,' Aaron pushed on. 'It's killing the fish.'

The tall man narrowed his eyes. 'And what's that to you?'

Grace caught her breath, not liking his sudden change of tone. 'Otters live here,' she said quickly. 'Otters are protected, and they need fish to eat.'

'So we're killing the otters as well, are we?'

'Not yet.'

'Then what's the problem?'

Chainsaw man sniggered, and another worker rolled his eyes. Anger bubbled up inside Grace. It was clear that the foreman was being deliberately difficult.

Taking a deep breath, she tried again to explain. 'If all the fish die, then the otters, and lots of other animals who live by the river, won't have enough food, and they might die too.'

'Right so. Quite the little conservationist, aren't you?' the tall man said, scowling. 'Get lost. We've got work to do.'

Grace took a deep breath to calm herself, but she couldn't hold her temper any longer. 'And you should clear up your litter!' she exploded.

Surprise flashed across the man's face, and he threw back his head and laughed. 'This land is private. You shouldn't even be here, so go away out of it with your ponies.'

The chainsaw man waved his machine at them for good measure. Nipper's ears flicked back, and the pony stepped away. 'That's right, get out of here!' said the man, and he took a threatening step towards them.

At first, Grace held her ground, but as the workmen came closer her courage failed. She looked over at Aaron, who was speaking calmly to Nipper. He shook his head at her, and Grace guessed he was thinking the same thing. It was time to leave. She gathered up her reins, but before she could ask Daisy to walk on, the taller man broke into a run.

'I *said* get out of here!' he roared.

'Go!' Aaron wheeled Nipper around and pushed him into a canter.

Grace pushed Daisy after him. Twigs snagged at her clothes, and she threw herself forwards over Daisy's neck to avoid the low-hanging branches as they raced away. Behind her, she could hear feet pounding and jeers as the workmen gave chase.

'Go!' she urged Daisy, pushing her on. Grace's heart thundered inside her chest. What would happen if the men caught them? 'Faster!' She gave Daisy her head. The mare pounded on, chasing Nipper and almost unseating Grace as she swerved round a tree. Grace caught a glimpse of the river. They were almost back on the greenway. Then Daisy's stride faltered, and she

suddenly stumbled. Grace recovered her balance and
patted Daisy's neck. 'Good girl.' Daisy's gait became
uneven again, and Grace realised that the pony was
limping. Immediately, she pulled up, glancing nervously
behind her as she did so. But the woods were quiet and
empty. The workmen seemed to have melted away.

Sighing with relief, Grace called out to Aaron,
'Wait up!'

Aaron waved a hand to show he'd heard her,
but he was clearly struggling with Nipper. Eventually,

Nipper slowed enough for Aaron to turn him back.
Grace dismounted, looping Daisy's reins over her
head and running her hand down the pony's foreleg.
There were no knocks or bumps she could feel, so she
asked Daisy to lift her hoof. Obediently, Daisy lifted a
leg, leaning into Grace and nibbling her hair as Grace
examined the hoof. She'd expected to find a stone
trapped in the metal horseshoe but was shocked to
see a nail lodged at the top of the V-shaped part of the
hoof. Blood seeped from the wound.

'Ouch!' Grace winced, guessing how painful that would feel. Carefully, she gave the nail a wiggle to see if she could pull it out, but it was firmly embedded. She gently released Daisy's hoof and stroked the pony's neck.

'What happened?' asked Aaron, riding up.

'Daisy trod on a nail. I can't get it out.'

'Let's have a look.' Aaron dismounted and handed his reins to Grace before asking Daisy to lift her hoof for him. 'Ooh, nasty!' Pinching the head of the nail between his thumb and finger, Aaron tried to remove it too. 'It's not budging,' he said eventually.

'Daisy can't walk on it,' said Grace emphatically. It would be too painful to ask her to hobble all the way home, and anyway, walking on the nail could cause a bigger injury.

'We need a first aid kit,' said Aaron.

They stared at each other, both knowing what that meant.

Grace was first to break the silence. 'How are we going to get one? We don't have mobiles so we can't ring Grandad or Gabriela, and we're not allowed to separate. We promised that we'd always stay together.'

'We don't have another option,' said Aaron.

Conflicting thoughts clashed in Grace's head. It was clear that someone, probably Aaron, would have to ride home for help. But what would Grandad say about that? He'd been very clear. If they didn't stick together, then he'd stop them from riding out on their own. Grace was enjoying riding independently at last, especially jumping in the Furzebush Field. She didn't want to have to go back to being supervised by Gabriela or Grandad.

'You really can't make Daisy walk with a nail in her foot. It will make it worse,' said Aaron.

'I know,' Grace said, nodding. Aaron didn't have to remind her of the risks of Daisy putting weight on an injured hoof. 'What, then?' she whispered. 'Should we tie the ponies up here and run back? It wouldn't take us long!' Immediately she shook her head. 'Bad idea! We can't leave the ponies alone in the woods.'

'I'm riding back to the stables for help,' said Aaron decisively.

'But—'

Aaron interrupted. 'What else can we do? Daisy's more important than anything else.'

Grace smiled gratefully. Aaron was the best friend ever. She hoped Grandad wouldn't tell him off. She didn't *think* he would, Grandad was a big softie at heart. But he *had* been very clear about staying together. She just didn't know.

Aaron led Nipper closer so that Grace could help give him a leg up. Nipper needed a little bit of encouragement to walk away from Daisy. He let out a shrill whinny in protest as Aaron pushed him forward.

'I'm going to ride over the fields. It'll be faster than the greenway. See you soon,' Aaron shouted over his shoulder.

The woods suddenly seemed very quiet. Grace wrapped her arms around Daisy, taking comfort from her sweet pony smell. Daisy whickered softly into her hair. The pony stood awkwardly, her foreleg bent to avoid putting weight on her injured hoof.

'Be brave,' Grace said, stroking Daisy's face. 'Help's on the way,' she added, trying to convince herself as well as Daisy.

Chapter 12

Grace liked to be busy, and helplessly standing around in the woods made her feel like she was failing Daisy. Maybe there was something she could do to make her pony more comfortable. Grace asked Daisy to lift her leg so she could take another look, trying to reassure her as she did so. 'Don't worry, Aaron will be back soon – hopefully with Gabriela.'

Gabriela got on well with Grandad, and Grace hoped the student instructor might put in a good word for her and Aaron. Then maybe they could persuade Grandad, instead of removing their privileges completely, to only stop them riding out alone for a week or two.

Grace examined Daisy's foot again, and this time she noticed that the nail was shiny and new. That was good. It lessened the risk of infection. Without knowing how long the nail was, it was impossible to say whether it had damaged any tendons or other important parts of Daisy's foot. The blood had congealed around the entry point. Grace searched her pockets for a tissue and found three folded neatly together. Daisy turned her head and nudged Grace, whickering for a treat. Grace stroked the pony's nose. 'You're not hurting that much if you're still looking for snacks,' she chuckled. 'You can have a mint when I've finished. But only if you stand still!'

As if she understood, Daisy nodded her head. She didn't move an inch as Grace carefully cleaned the blood from her hoof.

Grace sighed. She was concerned that Daisy might get an infection. There were all sorts of nasty things lurking on the forest floor, most of them too small to see. Suddenly, Grace had an idea. Gently putting Daisy's hoof down, she pulled the scrunchie from the end of her plait and examined it. It was an old one, and, as Grace hoped, a stitch of thread was loose. Grace picked at the stitch with her fingernail, worrying at it until it began to unravel. Soon, the stitch was large enough for her to get her little finger underneath it. Grace snapped the thread and pulled one of the broken ends. As the stitching unravelled, the material peeled back, revealing a band of elastic in the middle of the scrunchie. Grace grinned. 'Right, Daisy, I'm making you a temporary bandage,' she said.

Solemnly, Daisy turned her big, brown eyes on Grace and nuzzled the girl's cheek with her whiskery nose.

'I know, I love you too. You really are the best pony in the world,' said Grace, stroking her. Then she deftly folded the two remaining tissues into a pad to cover the inside of Daisy's hoof. Using the scrunchie material for a bandage, she covered the hoof with it. There was just enough. Holding the material in place, Grace tried to fix the piece of elastic around the edge of Daisy's hoof to hold everything in place. At first, it didn't seem like the elastic would stretch that far, but as she worked it the elastic slowly loosened. At last, it was big enough to encompass Daisy's whole hoof. With the makeshift bandage firmly in place, Grace gave Daisy a mint. The pony ate quickly, nudging Grace for another, then another, and when Grace finally stopped feeding her, Daisy's head drooped with disappointment.

The loneliness of the woods was beginning to get to Grace. Nervously, she looked about.

How long had Aaron been gone? She wished she'd thought to check what time he'd left. It seemed an eternity ago. Grandad always stressed the importance of treating a wound quickly to stop the risk of infection. It was especially crucial with a hoof. Should she try to walk Daisy home now she'd bandaged her? But if the nail was embedded a long way into the hoof, then walking on it would definitely make it worse. And what if Grace went back and missed everyone because they'd gone a different way to get back to her and Daisy? No, it was best to stay put, she decided.

Suddenly, Daisy lifted her head, her ears swivelling.

'What is it, girl?' Grace stared through the trees. She couldn't see anyone, but then she heard a distant whinny. It sounded like Nipper. Daisy clearly thought so too and whinnied back. Grace felt a huge jolt of relief, especially when she heard the snapping of twigs and the jingle of a horse's bridle. Help was here!

A minute later, Aaron and Nipper rode towards her with Grandad riding alongside on Storm.

'You're back,' called Grace, waving at them.

'That we are!' said Grandad, dismounting. He handed his reins to Aaron, who had also dismounted, and then took some pliers and a first aid kit from his saddle bag.

He went over to Daisy. 'What have we got here, then?' he asked, calmly. Handing the pliers and first aid kit to Grace, he ran a hand down Daisy's leg, stopping at the makeshift bandage and inspecting it.

'Lift up. Good girl,' he muttered, as Daisy gave him her hoof. Carefully, Grandad unpeeled the bandage. 'That's a very bold nail. Let's see if we can remove it. But first, I'll take some pictures for the vet so we can find the entry site again.' Grandad brought out his mobile and took several pictures of the nail from different angles. 'That should do it. Right, would you give me the pliers?'

Grace passed them over. She wasn't squeamish when it came to injuries, and she watched with

interest as Grandad carefully eased the nail from Daisy's hoof. Daisy's ears flicked back, and she rolled her eyes, showing the whites. Grace stroked her neck, talking to her in a calm voice the whole time.

'Will you look at that!' Holding the nail in the pliers, Grandad showed it to Grace and Aaron. 'It's a good thing not to have that in her hoof a moment longer. I'll put a poultice on the hoof before we walk her back to the stables. I've already called the veterinary surgery, and they're sending Roisin out. She's in the area.'

Grace felt a rush of relief. She liked Roisin, who loved horses and had three of her own. Grandad flipped open the first aid kit and pulled out a clear jar filled with a sticky, white paste, a spatula, a lint pad and some blue bandages. Grace recognised the paste as one Grandad made himself with Epsom salts. She'd seen him use it before on his horses to draw infection out of a wound. Standing with his back to Daisy's head, Grandad tucked her hoof between his legs.

He smeared a generous amount
of the paste onto the lint pad
and held it against the hoof.

'Put your finger right there,' he said to Grace.

Obediently, Grace held the lint in place with a
finger. Daisy's lips brushed her head as she tried to
see what Grace was doing.

'Nosy!' said Grace affectionately.

Deftly, Grandad bandaged the whole hoof,
keeping the blue bandage flat and not pulling it too
tight on Daisy's leg, especially above the sensitive
coronary band, where the hair met the top of the
hoof. Grace nodded her approval. When the hoof was
bandaged, Grandad fixed it in place with the sticky
strap and slid two fingers inside to check it wasn't
pinching. 'That's grand! Let's see if she can walk on
it now.'

'Come on, girl.' Grace moved off, clicking her
tongue in encouragement. She was thrilled when
Daisy went with her.

'That's it. Nice and slow,' said Grandad. 'Aaron, you ride Nipper at the back. Shout if you need me to stop.'

Grace breathed a huge sigh of relief as the group set off. Daisy had a proper bandage, and the vet was on her way. Grace's lips twitched into a smile as she glanced back at Aaron, plodding behind her on Nipper. But he was lost in thought and didn't notice her. Grace wanted to ask him how Grandad had reacted when Aaron had arrived at the stables alone, and whether he'd had a chance to tell Grandad about the men polluting the river. But there wasn't time now. A wave of unease washed over Grace. She'd have to wait for the vet to leave before she discovered how much trouble the two of them were actually in.

Chapter 13

As Grace and Aaron followed Grandad into the yard, they were met by Aleksy, who jumped down from the post and rail fence he'd been sitting on, waiting for them. Gabriela was sweeping the yard, but she stopped, propped up her broom and came over too.

'Go away out of that,' said Grace, blushing. 'Why are you both still here?'

It was late. Lessons had finished for the day, and the yard was very quiet.

'We were worried about you,' said Aleksy. 'I called my mam to ask if I could stay until you got back. Is Daisy OK?'

'I think so,' said Grace cautiously. 'The nail was clean, and it wasn't too big.'

'I'll bring her an apple tomorrow,' Aleksy promised.

'Thanks.' Grace was filled with happiness. Rowan Tree Stables was her favourite place in the world, not just for the ponies, but for the amazing friends she made there.

A car trundled slowly along the drive. 'That's Roisin now,' said Grandad. 'Someone take Storm for me.'

Aleksy ran over to lead Storm away. The gelding was a bit of a comedian in the stables, known for tricks like leaning on the groom, or picking a linen stable rubber up between his teeth and dropping it on their head. Everyone loved him for it, but right now

144

even he seemed to have picked up on the seriousness of the situation, because he followed Aleksy calmly.

Aaron took Nipper back to his stable, and Grace took Daisy back to hers while Grandad went to greet the vet. Gabriela followed, helpfully putting their tack away while Grace and Aaron brushed their ponies down.

Grandad appeared with Roisin just as Grace was putting a headcollar on Daisy to make it easier for the vet to examine her. Roisin checked Daisy's legs, running her hand down them, then undid Grandad's poultice to look at the wound. 'Good man, that poultice is working a treat.'

'All right, sweetheart,' she said to Daisy, stroking the pony's neck. 'We'll soon have you fixed up.'

Roisin turned to Grace. 'As far as I can tell, the damage is minimal. The poultice can stay on. I'll give her a tetanus injection to stop any possible infection and a painkiller to mix into her feed. Rest her for a few days, and she'll soon be back working again.'

'Thanks so much, Roisin. Did you hear that, Daisy?' Grace asked. She arranged Daisy's wavy, grey mane with her fingers until it all lay on the same side and then she patted her. 'You're going to be fine.' She sighed with relief.

It was time for the evening stables routine, and in no time at all the horses were fed, watered and bedded down for the night with bulging hay nets. Grace leaned on Daisy's stable door, watching her pony steadily munching on the sweet-smelling hay. She seemed none the worse for her adventure.

'See you tomorrow!' Aleksy called, waving as he headed out of the yard.

'Bye,' said Aaron, who'd been saying goodnight to Nipper.

'I won't forget that apple,' Aleksy called back.

'Grand! See you tomorrow,' said Grace.

Grace and Aaron were just leaving the barn when Gabriela arrived with a bunch of keys to lock up. 'Your grandad's gone home. He said he'll see you both there.'

Grace and Aaron exchanged a look. This was the second time that Grandad had summoned them in two weeks. The first time, it was to give them good news. Grace knew better than to expect the same again. They'd broken a promise, and now they had to face the consequences.

'Sure, I'd do it all over again,' said Aaron as if reading her mind. 'It's not like we've got mobiles. What else were we supposed to do?'

Grace nodded. No matter how many times she'd thought about it during evening stables, she knew that she wouldn't have done anything differently. 'Did you tell Grandad about the tree felling?' she asked.

Aaron nodded. 'He said he'd sort it.'

They collected their bikes and cycled the short distance down the drive to Rowan House. Leaving their bikes at the gate, they walked up the path. Grace rang the doorbell and waited as its chimes set off frantic barking. Granny opened the door, and Rocky dived between her legs, almost tripping her up as he flung himself at Grace and Aaron.

'Rocky, stop acting the maggot,' said Aaron, gently pushing him down as the little dog jumped up at him.

'Hiya, Granny! How are you?' Grace gave her grandmother a hug.

'Better for seeing you, darling. Come straight through to the garden. Your grandad and I were just having a cup of tea. Would you like a drink?'

'Better not,' said Grace. 'Mam's expecting me back for dinner.'

'Grandad's already called her and explained that you'll be late. He rang your parents too, Aaron,' she added. 'Now, come and have a seat and a drink. You've a story to tell by the sounds of it!'

Aaron raised his eyebrows at Grace, and she returned the look. That didn't sound too good.

They went through the kitchen to the back garden. Grandad was sitting at the patio table with a pot of tea and two mugs. He drew his gaze back from the fields where the Connemara ponies were grazing and pulled out chairs for them. As she threw herself down on a chair, Grace noticed her grandad's brow was wrinkled with frown lines. Aaron spotted a tennis ball under the table and threw it for Rocky before sitting down next to Grace. Rocky chased after it, diving into the flower bed as the ball rolled under a shrub.

Then Granny arrived with red lemonade and a plate of delicious-looking buttercream-topped cupcakes.

Grace recognised them as coming from the bakery in Greenfort. She took a sip of the ice-cold lemonade, but her stomach was churning too violently to manage a cake.

Grandad sighed. 'Don't look so worried. Your otters are safe. I rang the Environmental Protection Agency before I came to rescue you, while Gabriela tacked up Storm for me. They were very concerned to hear about the effects of the tree felling on the river. They weren't aware that there were otters at the location, and they're going to send someone to investigate immediately. They've promised to keep me informed of developments. They were very impressed with you both, for noticing the pollution and for trying to find out where it came from. But they asked that next time you find a problem as big as that, you report it to them first.'

'That's great!' Grace felt some of the tension leave her, and she knew from Aaron's huge grin that he was thrilled too.

Grandad reached for the teapot and topped up his mug. Grace wriggled in her seat. Now she'd had the good news, she wanted to get the bad over and done with. 'It was my fault that Aaron left me in the woods. I made him ride back alone. I didn't want to move Daisy in case it made her hoof worse.'

Grandad interrupted before Grace could say anymore. 'Did you think I was cross with you for that?'

When Grace and Aaron both nodded, he sank his head in his hands. 'Come on! When I said you were to stick together, I meant you weren't allowed to ride off alone because you'd had a disagreement or wanted to do different things. What I should have said was, don't go riding off alone *unless* there are exceptional circumstances! I'm very proud of you both, actually. Granny is too.'

'That I am!' said Granny.

'You are?' Grace and Aaron stared at each other in disbelief.

'It wasn't your fault that Daisy picked up a nail. You both did exactly the right thing. You used your initiative. The same can be said for the pollution problem. You'd mentioned it to me, and in one respect I'm to blame for not investigating it sooner. The only thing I will say is, next time don't go talking to strangers. As you found out, some of them aren't very friendly!'

'So we're not in any trouble?' asked Aaron.

'We can still ride out alone and go to the Furzebush Field?' Grace added.

'Of course!' said Grandad.

Grace jumped up, almost knocking her chair over as she ran round the patio cheering wildly, before stopping to hug both Grandad and Granny.

'Thanks, Denis.' Aaron couldn't stop beaming.

'Let's go to the Furzebush Field tomorrow!' said Grace. Her face fell suddenly when she remembered that Daisy was lame. But she didn't mind waiting. Roisin seemed to think that Daisy would recover quickly, and with the lighter evenings there'd soon be plenty of time for riding and jumping.

'Have a chat with Gabriela,' said Grandad. 'We've plenty of ponies. I'm sure she can spare a different one.'

'Thanks, Grandad.' Grace was suddenly starving. She took a cake as she sat down. Rocky's head popped up from the flowerbed. Grace paused with the cake halfway to her mouth. 'What's Rocky got there?'

The little dog looked like he was fighting with a long, green snake. Grace stared at the floppy thing clamped between Rocky's jaws, and then she snorted with laughter. 'Hey, Aaron, is that your sock?'

'What?' Aaron's head whipped round. 'The little rascal!' he groaned. 'Did he bury it in the garden?'

Rocky looked mighty pleased with himself as he padded closer, dragging the mud-stained sock behind him.

'Thanks, Rocky,' said Aaron. 'My teacher made me borrow a smelly old sock from lost property to wear for hurling today because of you.'

Grace couldn't stop laughing. 'It could have been worse. At least he didn't steal your pants!'

'What's this about? Has Rocky been thieving again?' Grandad went over to retrieve the sock and ended up chasing Rocky around the garden. Aaron joined in, and Grace collapsed in giggles as the chase ended in a tug of war. While Aaron and Rocky both pulled on different ends of the sock, Grandad crept up behind the Jack Russell. Grabbing the little terrier's collar with one hand, he teased the sock free with his other hand and gave it back to Aaron.

'Er, thanks. I think,' said Aaron, gingerly holding the soggy sock between his thumb and a finger.

Grace bit into the cupcake, sighing happily as she swallowed the first delicious mouthful. 'Now that the otters are safe, we can look forward to having fun with the ponies without worrying.'

'And maybe another adventure,' said Aaron, putting his sock on the table out of Rocky's reach.

'*Definitely* another adventure,' Grace agreed. 'Bring it on!'

Glossary

Bay: A bay horse has a black mane and tail, and black lower legs. Its body can be any shade of brown.

Coronary band: At the top of the hoof. It makes the horn that forms the hoof wall.

Cross-country riding: A horse race, over jumps or obstacles, across the countryside.

D-ring: A D-shaped ring on a saddle used to fasten an object to it, such as a water bottle.

Dun: A dun horse has a black mane, tail and legs. Its body can be any shade, from mouse-brown to gold.

Foreleg: The front leg of a horse.

Gelding: A neutered male horse.

Girth: A broad strap of material that goes round a horse's belly to keep the saddle in place. It can be made from cotton, webbing or leather.

Hack: To ride a horse out from where it is kept, usually across the countryside.

Hands: Sometimes referred to as 'hands high', this is how a horse's height is measured. The measurement is taken from the ground to the withers (base of the neck).

Headcollar: This is a kind of halter that is made of nylon, rope or leather and secured with a buckle. It is put on a horse's head and when a lead rope is attached, the horse can be easily led.

Piebald: A piebald horse has black and white patches.

Sand school: An enclosed ring where horses and their riders can practise riding.

Socks: A horse is said to have socks when it has white hair on the lower part of its leg below the knee.

Skewbald: A skewbald horse has brown and white patches.

Stable rubber: A cloth used after grooming to polish the horse's coat. They are often made from linen.

Stirrups: Stirrups are attached to the saddle and are for the rider to put their feet in. They are usually made of metal but can also be made from strong plastic.

Tack: The equipment used to ride a horse, such as a saddle and bridle.

Triathlon: A race consisting of cycling, swimming and running.

Withers: The ridge, at the base of the horse's neck, between the horse's shoulder blades. It is the tallest point of the body.